AF228158

EXPLORING NATURE

Spotting Rocks

BY EMILY HECK

Kids Core
An Imprint of Abdo Publishing
abdobooks.com

abdobooks.com

Published by Abdo Publishing, a division of ABDO, PO Box 398166, Minneapolis, Minnesota 55439. Copyright © 2026 by Abdo Consulting Group, Inc. International copyrights reserved in all countries. No part of this book may be reproduced in any form without written permission from the publisher. Kids Core™ is a trademark and logo of Abdo Publishing.

Printed in the United States of America, North Mankato, Minnesota.
102025
012026

THIS BOOK CONTAINS RECYCLED MATERIALS

Cover Photo: Shutterstock Images
Interior Photos: Shutterstock Images, 4–5, 7, 12–13, 17 (top left), 17 (middle left), 17 (bottom left), 17 (middle), 17 (bottom middle), 17 (top right), 17 (middle right), 17 (bottom right), 25, 28 (top right), 28 (bottom left), 28 (bottom right); James St. John/Flickr, 6; Monkey Business Images/Shutterstock Images, 8; Damian Pawlos/Shutterstock Images, 10; Ralf Lehmann/Shutterstock Images, 14; Aleksandr Pobedimskiy/Shutterstock Images, 17 (top middle); Eric Poulin/Shutterstock Images, 18; Pornpimon Ainkaew/Shutterstock Images, 20–21; Inna Reznik/Shutterstock Images, 22; Minakryn Ruslan/Shutterstock Images, 23; iStockphoto, 26; Irina Gutyryak/Shutterstock Images, 28 (top left)

Editor: Marie Pearson
Series Designer: Marley Richmond

Library of Congress Control Number: 2025939177

Publisher's Cataloging-in-Publication Data

Names: Heck, Emily, author.
Title: Spotting rocks / by Emily Heck
Description: Minneapolis, Minnesota: Abdo Publishing, 2026 | Series: Exploring nature | Includes online resources and index.
Identifiers: ISBN 9781098298739 (lib. bdg.) | ISBN 9798384932536 (ebook)
Subjects: LCSH: Rocks--Juvenile literature. | Rock collectors--Juvenile literature. | Geoscience (Geology)--Juvenile literature. | Nature--Juvenile literature. | Ecological science--Juvenile literature. | Habitats (Ecology)--Juvenile literature.
Classification: DDC 552.0--dc23

CONTENTS

Streams can be good places
to find rocks.

CHAPTER 1

Treasure Everywhere

Harper is playing in the creek in her grandpa's backyard. Something catches her eye. She picks it up out of the shallow water. It's a rock. She looks at it closely. The rock is a reddish-brown color. When it dries, it shimmers in the sunlight.

Harper shows the rock to her grandpa. He knows a lot about rocks. Her grandpa looks at the rock with a magnifying glass. He says it is a piece of quartzite. Its **crystals** make it shiny.

Harper asks her grandpa if she can keep it. He smiles and says yes. Harper decides she wants to start a rock collection. She can't wait to find more treasures in her own backyard!

Quartzite is usually white or gray. However, iron can stain it red.

Mountains are made of very large pieces of rock.

Rocks All Around

Rocks can be found almost anywhere on Earth.

Some rocks are buried deep underground.

Others lie on Earth's surface.

People may look for rocks on beaches. Waves often wash new rocks onto the shore.

Rocks are found on beaches and in riverbeds. They make up mountains. People use rocks for **landscaping** in yards.

Many people enjoy searching for rocks. This is called rockhounding. People might rockhound to find gemstones or valuable rocks.

Other people rockhound to explore the outdoors. It helps them learn new things about the world around them.

Always Changing

Rocks are made of minerals. A mineral is a substance found in nature. Minerals are not living. They are shaped like crystals. There are more than 5,800 known minerals. But new minerals are always being discovered.

Earth's Oldest Rock

Earth's **crust** is home to some very old rocks. The oldest rock is in a part of the crust called the Canadian Shield, which is in Canada. This rock is called the Acasta Gneiss. It is about 4 billion years old.

Rocks come in many shapes, sizes, and textures.

Rocks form over time when a mineral or minerals pack together in a solid mass. This happens in different ways. Some rocks are shaped by heat and pressure. Other rocks are formed by water. Minerals collect in water.

Then the water evaporates, leaving behind a solid mass of minerals. All rocks have been a different type of rock at some point in time. As time goes on, rocks continue to change.

Rocks tell extraordinary stories. They can show what Earth was like long before humans were living on it. Finding and studying rocks is a great way to discover more about the world and its history.

Further Evidence

Look at the website below. Does it give any new evidence to support Chapter One?

Geology 101

abdocorelibrary.com/spotting-rocks

Sedimentary rock forms in layers. Sometimes the layers become exposed and are visible to the human eye.

CHAPTER 2

Looking for Rocks

It's helpful to learn more about rocks when rockhounding. Rocks are put into three categories. These are igneous, sedimentary, and metamorphic. These categories tell people how the rocks formed.

Igneous rocks form when melted rock cools. Melted rock is called magma. It becomes lava when it comes to Earth's surface through volcanoes. There are two types of igneous rock. Intrusive rocks cool under Earth's surface. Extrusive rocks cool on the surface. Examples of igneous rocks are obsidian, pumice, and granite.

Sedimentary rocks are made from small bits of other rocks. They can also be made from pieces of **organisms** that were once alive. Water moves these pieces around. They settle at the bottoms of lakes and oceans. Layers are created over time. The weight of the layers presses the material into solid rock. Shale, sandstone, and limestone are types of sedimentary rocks.

Metamorphic rocks form deep underground. They start as igneous or sedimentary rocks.

Finding Fossils

Sedimentary rocks can have fossils in their layers. Some fossils are parts of plants or animals that have turned to stone. Other fossils are imprints of plants or animals in stone. Fossils were buried thousands of years ago. Imprint fossils of leaves are common to find.

Heat, pressure, and other minerals turn them into metamorphic rocks. These processes pack minerals together more tightly. The processes can even change the original minerals into different kinds of minerals. Some types of metamorphic rocks are phyllite, quartzite, gneiss, and marble.

Finding and Taking

Rocks are easy to find. Beaches and rivers are good places to look. But people need to be careful when taking rocks. People can take rocks from some public land. But people cannot collect these rocks to sell. And people should not take rocks from protected land such as national parks.

Types of Rocks

There are many types of rocks people can search for.

It's good to bring some items along when rockhounding. A small backpack is helpful for carrying rocks. A notebook is also helpful. It lets people write down where they find rocks. It's important to stay safe outdoors as well. Gloves can protect the hands. Sunscreen and a water bottle are important. People should never go rockhounding alone. Children should go only with an adult's permission.

Dr. Kerry Griffis-Kyle is an ecology professor. She talks about taking rocks from public places:

> Most of the time it's okay to pick up a few rocks for personal use on **federal** land, but you can't pick up fossils and **artifacts**. And never pick up anything on Park Service or DOD (Department of Defense) land.

Source: "Rockhounding Women." *Rock & Gem Magazine*, 13 Nov. 2023, rockngem.com. Accessed 5 Mar. 2025.

Comparing Texts

Think about the quote. Does it support the information in this chapter? Or does it give a different perspective? Explain how in a few sentences.

Looking closely at rocks can help people determine their type.

Identifying Rocks

After collecting rocks, many people enjoy learning what they are. Rockhounds can start by learning what category a rock belongs to. Igneous rocks do not have layers. They can look smooth and shiny because their grains are small.

Sedimentary rocks can be many colors and may have fossils. Metamorphic rocks often sparkle.

A rock's color and **luster** help with identification. Its grain size, which is the size of each particle in the rock, also helps.

A magnifying glass is helpful for looking closely at rocks. Rocks can also be identified by testing their hardness. A pocketknife can help test hardness. These things tell people more about what the rock is made of.

The Mohs scale measures mineral hardness. Fire agates rate 6 to 7 on the scale, meaning a masonry drill bit will scratch them but a steel nail won't.

Field guides can help people identify rocks. A rock field guide is a book with many photos of rocks. It has information such as rock appearance and where different types of rocks are found. Geologists can help identify rocks too. These people study rocks. A museum or university is a good place to find a rock expert.

Hidden Gems

Minerals in rocks can form gemstones. Some gemstones are aquamarine, emerald, jade, and diamond. Agates are more common to find. They are a type of quartz. They can have colorful bands.

A label can be a small piece of paper, a sticker stuck to the rock, or a number written directly on the rock.

On Display

After identifying a rock, a rockhound can add a label. Each rock in a collection should have a number that can be put on the label.

A collector can write that number in a notebook. The notebook entry should say what type of rock it is. It can say when and where the rock was found.

Rockhounds often enjoy displaying their collections. Rocks can be put on a shelf. Or they may be put in a shadow box. These displays can inspire others to get outside so they can discover treasures in their neighborhoods too!

Field Notes

Magnifying glass

Backpack

Notebook

Gloves

Rock Log

Collection number:
17

Type of rock:
Igneous—obsidian

Location found:
Obsidian Tank at Government Mountain, Arizona

Date found:
April 3

Grain size:
Too small to see

Color:
Black

Luster:
Glassy

Mohs scale number (hardness):
5

Other description notes (fossils, crystals, transparency):
Does not let light through

A blank Rock Log is available at **abdocorelibrary.com.**

Glossary

artifacts
old things from an earlier period of time

crust
the outer layer of Earth

crystals
solid objects whose structures have a repeating pattern

federal
having to do with the central government of a country

landscaping
decorating a piece of land, such as by adding plants or rocks

luster
the shine of a surface

organisms
living things

Online Resources

To learn more about rocks and rockhounding, visit our free resource websites below.

Visit **abdocorelibrary.com** or scan this QR code for free Common Core resources for teachers and students, including vetted activities, multimedia, and booklinks, for deeper subject comprehension.

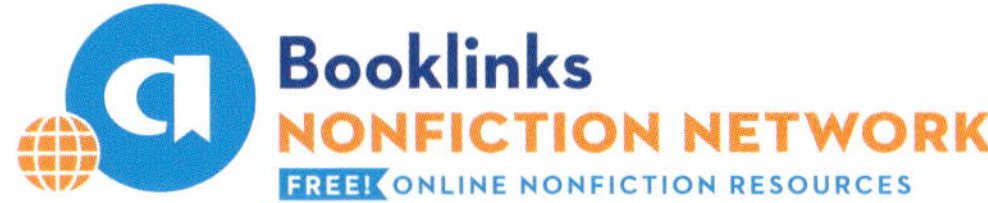

Visit **abdobooklinks.com** or scan this QR code for free additional online weblinks for further learning. These links are routinely monitored and updated to provide the most current information available.

Learn More

Marquardt, Meg. *Rocks and Minerals.* Abdo, 2025.

Trusiani, Lisa. *All About Rocks and Minerals.* Rockridge, 2021.

Wei-Haas, Maya. *What a Rock Can Reveal.* Phaidon, 2024.

Index

About the Author

Emily Heck is a freelance writer and editor in Minnesota. When she's not writing, she enjoys reading, crafting, and spending time outdoors.